More fabulous books
from Little Tiger Press!

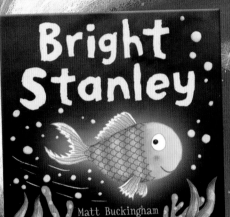

Bright
Stanley
Matt Buckingham

Bored Bill
Liz Pichon

Rhino's
Great
BIG
Itch!
Natalie Chivers

ouch!
Ragnhild Scamell   Michael Terry

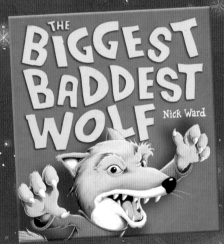

THE
BIGGEST
BADDEST
WOLF Nick Ward

A Little
Fairy Magic
Julia Hubery   Alison Edgson

For information regarding any of the above titles
or for our catalogue, please contact us:
Little Tiger Press, 1 The Coda Centre, 189 Munster Road, London SW6 6AW
Tel: 020 7385 6333 • E-mail: contact@littletiger.co.uk • www.littletiger.co.uk

Image taken from *Bored Bill* copyright © Liz Pichon 2005

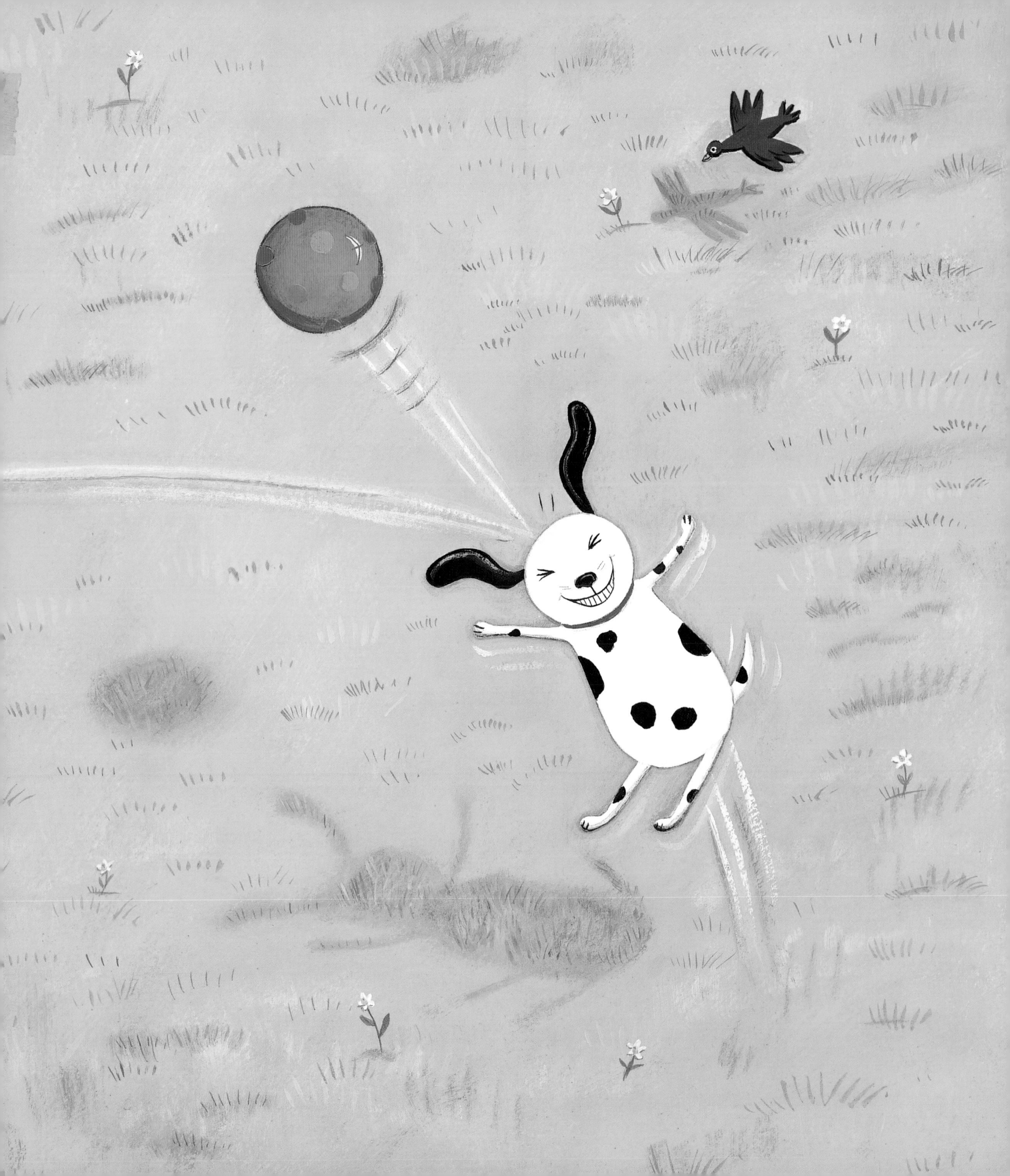

. . . especially when they
had so many new
friends round for tea!

So from that day on, Bill always kept himself busy, just like Mrs Pickle did. He read books and practised kung fu.

He dug the garden and cooked delicious food.

Bill even enjoyed doing the cleaning, which Mrs Pickle thought was very helpful . . .

. . . . MRS PICKLE!

"I'll never be bored again!" said
Bill as he hugged Mrs Pickle.

So the aliens brought out their spaceship and flew Bill back down to earth. They all waved and said goodbye.

When Bill landed he found he was FAMOUS!

EVERYONE wanted to talk to Bill about the aliens. But the only person Bill wanted to see was . . .

Bill cooked the aliens a lovely meal just like Mrs Pickle's.

He showed them some of Mrs Pickle's top kung fu moves.

Then they played some games, which everyone enjoyed.

"Come along!" Bill shouted to the aliens. "Boring aliens get bored. It's time to have some fun!"

Bill had never been so bored.
He really missed Mrs Pickle
and her delicious food.

So bored . . .

Bill looked at the aliens lying around the planet.
"Mrs Pickle was right!" he thought suddenly.
"Doing nothing all day is REALLY BORING!
We need to get BUSY."

But it wasn't. The squidgy green food was **REVOLTING!** Worse still, the aliens ate it for every single meal.

Life on the planet with the aliens was not very interesting at all. They just sat around all day long doing absolutely **NOTHING.**

"Fantastic!" thought Bill. "Alien food MUST be delicious."

Bill asked the aliens to show him the whole planet.
"LET'S EXPLORE AND HAVE FUN!" Bill shouted.
"What's the point of exploring?" the aliens sighed.
"Exploring is borrrring."
"I'm hungry," one alien mumbled. So they all
went to have some squidgy green food.

The noise woke up the aliens. They all popped up to see what it was. Bill was delighted to meet them. "This planet looks like fun," he smiled. "I bet Mrs Pickle isn't having an adventure like this!"

Meanwhile, back on EARTH, Mrs Pickle gets rescued . . .

THUMP!

Bill landed on a strange
purple planet.

and up into space he flew.

"AT LAST!" cheered Bill.
"No more boring walks for me.
Space will be REALLY
exciting."

Higher and higher he went. Faster and faster, past the moon and stars

Suddenly a huge gust of wind swept down and lifted them both off their feet.

"YIPPEEEE!" squealed Mrs Pickle as she disappeared from sight. Bill clung to a tree when SNAP! the branch broke and he was spun up into the air.

Outside the weather was dreadful.
It was cold and windy. It was so
windy that Mrs Pickle's hat flew off.
"Whoooops!" Mrs Pickle laughed.
"How borrring," groaned Bill.

"Come along, Bill, let's go for
a lovely long walk," Mrs Pickle said.
"Borrrrrring," muttered Bill.
"Boring dogs get bored," said Mrs Pickle.
"Besides, it's no fun sitting around all
day doing nothing."
"I won't go," said Bill firmly.

I'm not
moving . . .

Mrs Pickle also liked to do lots of cleaning.
"I'm so bored I can't even move," sighed Bill.

Bill's owner Mrs Pickle was never bored.
She liked to keep busy **ALL** day.

Mrs Pickle loved reading,
but Bill thought reading
was boring.

Mrs Pickle adored gardening.
Bill thought gardening was
very dull indeed.

Mrs Pickle was a fantastic cook and a kung fu expert.
"Try this, Bill, it's fun!" she said happily.
"Oh no," sighed Bill.

Bill was bored. He wasn't just a little
bit bored, he was **REALLY REALLY** bored.

Bored Bill

Liz Pichon

LITTLE TIGER PRESS
London

Dedicated to Bill Flannery . . .
who was never bored or boring
— L P

LITTLE TIGER PRESS
1 The Coda Centre, 189 Munster Road,
London SW6 6AW
www.littletiger.co.uk

First published in Great Britain 2005
This edition published 2006

A CIP catalogue record for this book is available
from the British Library

Printed in China • LTP/1800/1729/1016

10 9 8 7 6 5 4 3 2

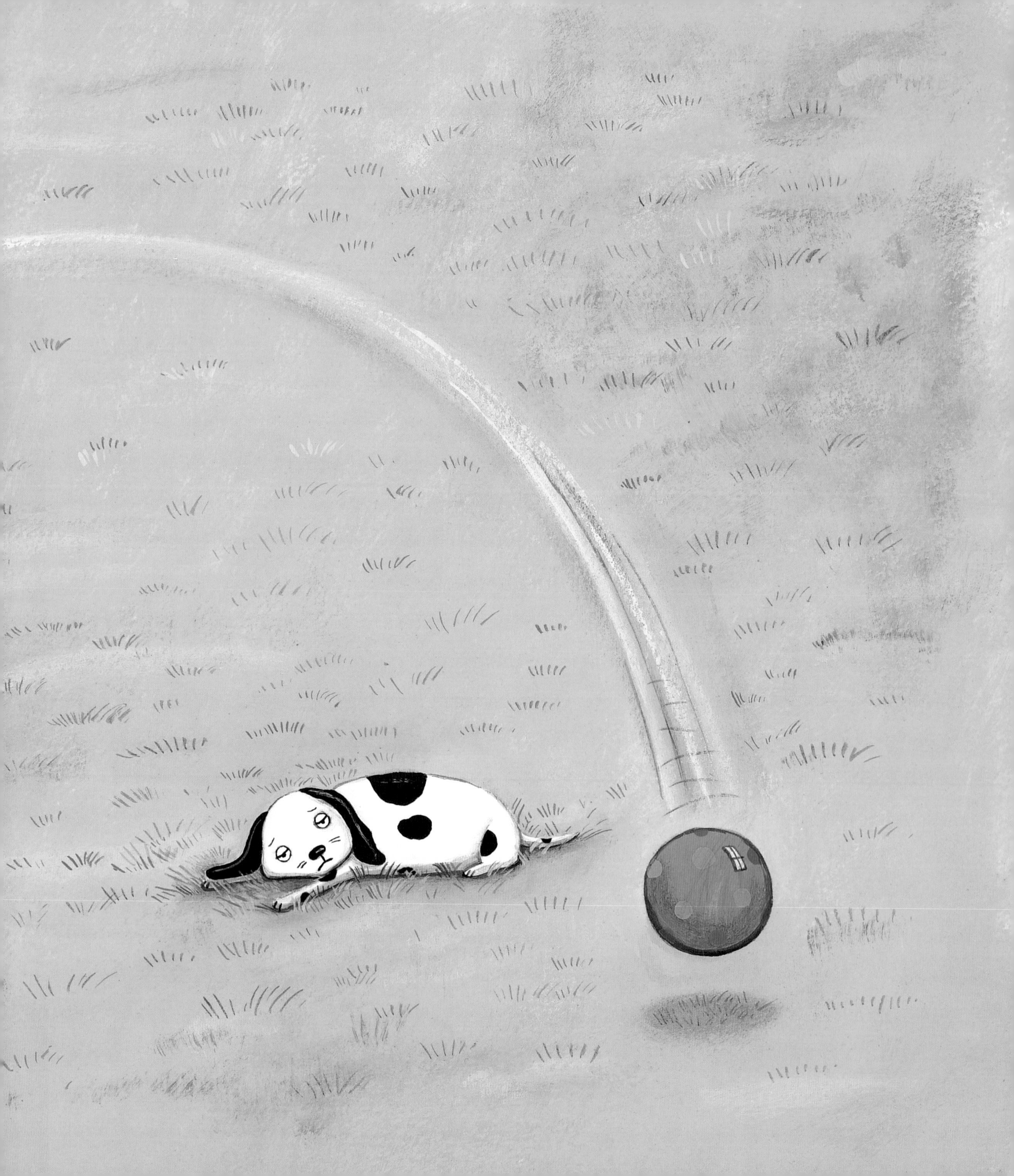

This Little Tiger book belongs to:

_____

_____

_____